Content note: this book contains adult themes.

First published in English in 2020 by Nobrow Ltd.
27 Westgate Street, London E8 3RL.

Originally published in French as L'Été Fantôme by Elizabeth Holleville.

Translation by Amy Evans-Hill.

1 3 5 7 9 10 8 6 4 2

Published in the US by Nobrow (US) Inc.

Printed in Poland on FSC® certified paper.

ISBN: 978-1-910620-72-4

www.nobrow.net

Elizabeth Holleville

SUMMER SPIRIT

Nobrow
London | New York

BRRRRRRR

RRRRRRRRR

WILL SOMEONE OPEN THE GATE?

GO ON, LOUISE!
I'LL DO IT, LYDIA, BUT NOT BECAUSE YOU TOLD ME TO!

HURRY UP!

GRRRR!
woof woof woof!

WOOF WOOF!

HAHA! HELLO, RODIN.

woof
woof!
SHH, QUIET DOWN ALREADY, RODIN!

WHEW, I'M MELTING IN THIS HEAT!
HI, MUM!

LET'S GO AND HAVE DRINKS ON THE BALCONY.

CAN I HELP YOU, GRANDMA?

NO, NO. I'LL BE FINE.

WHEN ARE THE COUSINS GETTING HERE?
TOMORROW.

sniff
sniff

MUM, SOMETHING IN YOUR KITCHEN SMELLS STRANGE...

I THINK IT'S COMING FROM HERE.

MEMO
UGH!

WHAT EVEN IS TH-

EW!

HOW ON EARTH DID YOU MANAGE TO PUT AN OLD CAMEMBERT IN WITH YOUR CLEAN DISHES AND FORGET ABOUT IT FOR THIS LONG?
CAREFUL WITH THAT TRAY, LYDIA!

IT WAS JUST SOME CHEESE!
I KNOW, BUT SHE'S NEVER DONE ANYTHING LIKE THAT BEFORE...

?

LOUISE.

WE'RE GOING IN HALF AN HOUR.
GO EASY ON YOUR GRANDMA, PLEASE!

NO SHENANIGANS, NO CLIMBING TREES! OKAY?
YES, MUM...

TICK
TOCK

TICK
TOCK

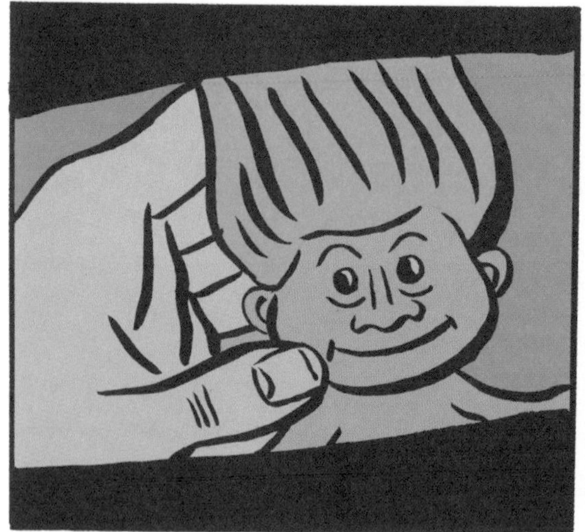

?

HAVE YOU SEEN MY TROLL?
NOPE. MAYBE RODIN TOOK IT?
HMM... DOESN'T SOUND LIKE HIM.

AREN'T YOU GETTING A BIT OLD FOR DOLLS, ANYWAY?

WOOF WOOF!

woof woof!
DO YOU EVER SHUT UP, YOU FILTHY MUTT?!

THEY'RE HERE!

ARGH, I FORGOT TO WAX! THIS REALLY SUCKS.

DO YOU WANT ME TO DO IT, SOPHIE?

WHAT I WANT IS TO ABOLISH WAXING IN SOCIETY ALTOGETHER. BUT, THE FACT IS, I'M NOT BRAVE ENOUGH TO GO TO THE BEACH WITH HAIRY LEGS. SO...
...IT LOOKS LIKE I HAVE TO DO IT ONE MORE TIME.

SPEAKING OF THE BEACH, WHY DON'T WE ALL GO WHILE IT'S STILL EARLY?
WAXING ISN'T THAT BAD, SOPHIE!
BIBA
SUMMER
AMAZING ANIMALS

RELAX, LOUISE, WE HAVE THE WHOLE SUMMER TO GO TO THE BEACH!

RRRRIP!
AGHH!

WANT TO PLAY CATCH, RODIN?
HMPF!

crunch
crunch

HA HA HA!

?

DAMN IT, RODIN!

UP FOR GOING TO THE BEACH, LOUISE?

MMM, THAT SMELLS SO GOOD!

DO YOU LIKE THE SMELL OF SUNSCREEN AS WELL?
I DO, BUT YOU SHOULD KNOW THAT IT KILLS FISH AND DAMAGES THE CORAL REEFS.

REALLY? THAT'S AWFUL...
OH MY GOD, MAUREEN, SUCH A KILLJOY!
HAHA! STOP IT!

WHO WANTS TO BUILD A SANDCASTLE?
NO, THANKS!

SOPHIE, DO YOU REMEMBER LAST SUMMER WHEN YOU DUG THAT REALLY DEEP DITCH?

OH YEAH!
IT WAS LIKE A BLACK HOLE!
DO YOU WANT TO MAKE ANOTHER ONE?

NAH, SORRY. I'M POOPED!
Flump!

LOOK, GIRLS — IT'S THAT HOT GUY FROM LAST SUMMER I TOLD YOU ABOUT.

HMM... THE SURFER GUY LOOK IN THE MEDITERRANEAN IS A BIT ABSURD...

BUT I ADMIT, HE IS PRETTY CUTE!
STOP LOOKING AT HIM LIKE THAT!
TAP TAP

SIGH
I DON'T STAND A CHANCE WITH THAT GUY...
SURE YOU DO.

LOUISE !!!
WHY DO YOU HAVE TO SCREAM AT HER LIKE THAT?

BECAUSE SHE DOES THIS EVERY TIME! AS SOON AS WE START CLEARING THE TABLE...

SHE SUDDENLY DISAPPEARS TO GO TO THE BATHROOM!
AMAZING ANIMALS
+200p

HOW COME YOU DIDN'T FEEL IT THERE?

OH... I DON'T KNOW... I'M GETTING OLD, HONEY.

GOOD NIGHT, GIRLS!
GOOD NIGHT, GRANDMA!
GOOD NIGHT!

GRANDMA?

WHO ARE THE LITTLE GIRLS IN THIS PHOTO?

THAT'S ME WITH MY OLDER SISTER... LISA.

YOU KNOW, IT'S STRANGE.

BUT WHENEVER I SEE THIS PICTURE...

I REMEMBER EVERYTHING ABOUT THAT SUMMER.
THE SMELL OF EUCALYPTUS AND THE TASTE OF FRESH PINE NUTS...

THE PRANKS WE PLAYED ON THE GROWN-UPS...

SIGH

THIS IS THE LAST PHOTO OUR DAD TOOK OF US.

POOR LISA...

DRIP, DROP. DRIP, DROP. THE YOUNG BOY HEARS THIS SOUND ALL NIGHT LONG.

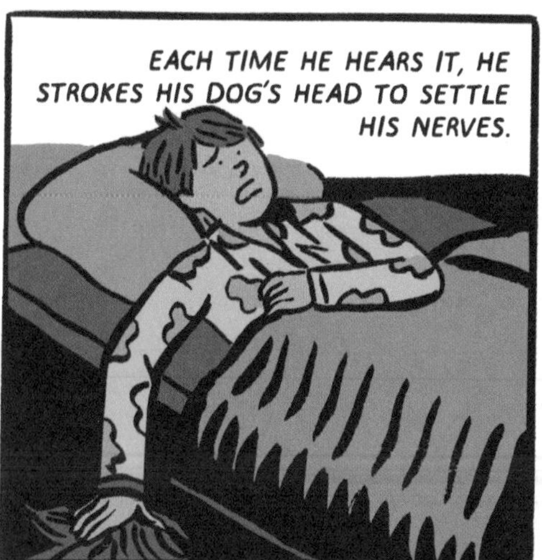
EACH TIME HE HEARS IT, HE STROKES HIS DOG'S HEAD TO SETTLE HIS NERVES.

WHEN HE CAN'T BEAR IT ANY MORE, HE DECIDES TO GO AND FOLLOW THE SOUND...
DRIP! DROP!

DRIP!
DROP!
ONLY TO DISCOVER, TO HIS HORROR, THAT WHAT HAD BEEN DRIPPING THIS WHOLE TIME – WAS THE SKINNED CORPSE OF HIS DOG! DRIP, DROP.

AND WHOSE HEAD WAS THE YOUNG BOY STROKING ALL THIS TIME, DO YOU THINK?

IT WAS THE MADMAN'S!
ARGH!

HAHA!

THAT WAS A PRETTY GOOD ONE. BUT GET READY FOR THE FRIGHT OF YOUR LIFE!

A KOREAN FRIEND OF MINE TOLD ME SOMETHING REALLY CREEPY...

IT WASN'T
JUST A STORY,
IT WAS MORE LIKE
A HOW-TO GUIDE...

...TO SEEING GHOSTS.

IT'S IMPOSSIBLE TO WATCH ALL FOUR CORNERS OF A ROOM AT THE SAME TIME...

AND THEY ALWAYS MOVE
SO THAT THEY'RE IN YOUR
BLIND SPOT...

TO TRICK THEM, WATCH EACH CORNER OF THE ROOM IN TURN, ALWAYS MOVING IN ONE DIRECTION...

THEN AT THE LAST SECOND, SPIN AROUND TO FACE THE OPPOSITE WAY.

YOU'LL CATCH A GLIMPSE OF YOUR GHOST...

WHO WON'T HAVE THE CHANCE TO HIDE.

GAH! I'LL NEVER CATCH HIS ATTENTION WITH ALL THESE PEOPLE AROUND...!

WELL, WHAT ARE YOU WAITING FOR? HE'S GOING TO THE SHOWERS!
YEAH?!

UNTZE
UNTZE
UNTZE

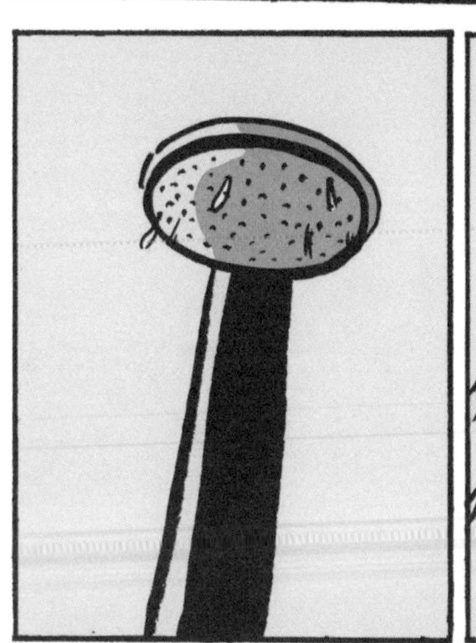

GIRLS,
LET'S GO OUT TONIGHT!

GRANDMA, CAN YOU TELL US THE STORY ABOUT THE RAT?
BUT YOU KNOW IT BY HEART!
WE DON'T MIND.
FINE, OKAY...

SO, WHEN I WAS VERY YOUNG AND I LIVED WITH MY FAMILY IN TUNISIA...

YOU HAD TO WALK ACROSS THE VILLAGE TO GET TO THE TOILETS.

IN THESE TOILETS...

THERE WAS A GAP BETWEEN THE GROUND AND THE DOOR.

ONE DAY WHEN I WAS DAYDREAMING, MINDING MY OWN BUSINESS...

I LOOKED DOWN AND SAW...

...A HUGE RAT!
CALMLY STANDING ON HIS HIND LEGS.

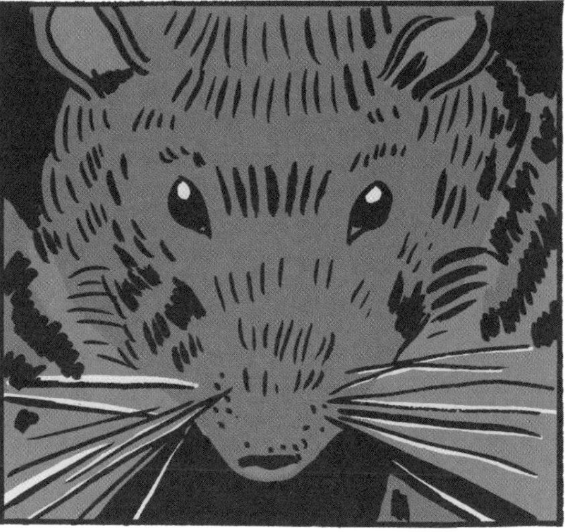

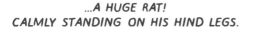

IT WASN'T SO MUCH THE RAT THAT FRIGHTENED ME, BUT HOW INTENSELY HE LOOKED AT ME – ALMOST LIKE A HUMAN.

SO WHAT DID YOU DO?

I SLOWLY MOVED TO THE EDGE OF THE TOILET...

...AND LEAPED OVER HIM, PUSHING OPEN THE DOOR!

THE RAT DIDN'T EVEN MOVE AN INCH WHILE I WAS RUNNING AWAY.

Rustle!
Rustle!

Swif!

HERE'S ONE THAT'S SCARED OF US!

GRANNYYYY?
OH, YOU!
I JUST KNOW YOU'RE
GOING TO ASK ME FOR
SOMETHING...

PLEASE, CAN WE GO AND
HAVE ICE CREAM ON THE
HARBOUR?

AH! I THOUGHT
THIS MIGHT START
HAPPENING AT
YOUR AGE!

WHAT TIME WILL YOU BE BACK?
MIDNIGHT?

BAR
DISCOTHÈQUE
LE SOLEIL

COCKTAIL
MOJITO 7€
BEACH MARY 6€

SO WE'RE NOT GOING FOR ICE CREAM?

UH, DUH!

A BEER, PLEASE.
AND... A HALF FOR ME.

I'LL HAVE A HALF, TOO!

THAT'S NOT GOING TO HAPPEN! YOU'LL HAVE A COKE.

ERR... HOW OLD ARE YOU GIRLS, EXACTLY?

I'M EIGHTEEN...

OH REALLY?
CAN I SEE YOUR ID?

WE FORGOT THEM.
PFFFFF!

PALM BAR
THANKS A LOT, LOUISE!
WHAT DID I DO?!

LOOK OVER THERE!

BOM

BOM

ISN'T THAT THE HOT GUY YOU LIKE?

HEY!
CAN WE SIT WITH YOU?
YEAH, SURE!
BOM! BOM!

HI.
WHAT'S YOUR NAME?
LYDIA.

AND WHAT'S YOURS?

IT'S MAUREEN, PLEASE DON'T MAKE ANY JOKES.
OH, I WOULDN'T DARE!

MY NAME'S HUMPHREY...
HAHA!
YOU'RE KIDDING?

I WISH I WAS.

MY MUM'S A BIG FAN OF THE FILM "CASABLANCA".

DO YOU WANT A DRAW?
YEAH.

Tap!
Tap

BUT THAT FILM SUCKS!

WHAT?
I WANT TO GO HOME.

HANG ON, SO YOU HAVE US DOING YOUR BIDDING ALL DAY...
THANKS!
BUT I'LL ADMIT THE HEROINE IN IT WAS PRETTY WELL DONE!

AND NOW MADAME WOULD LIKE TO LEAVE!
I THOUGHT WE WERE JUST GOING FOR AN ICE CREAM!

IT'S FINE, I'LL JUST GO BACK ALONE.

YOU WHAT?! GO BACK
ALONE??

WHOA. IS THAT HOW YOU TALK TO YOUR LITTLE SISTER?

OH, NOOO...

WOOF
WOOF!
SHHHHHH!

woof woof!

WILL SOMEONE SHUT THAT DOG UP?!
woof!

WHERE ARE YOU GOING?

psshh
hhhhhhh
Psh
hh

DON'T WORRY!
I'M NOT GOING TO HURT YOU.

I SUPPOSE YOU DON'T REALLY WANT TO BE TALKING TO A GHOST.

IT'S JUST THAT I'VE BEEN SO BORED IN THIS HOUSE ALL YEAR...

AND SINCE YOU AND YOUR COUSINS ARRIVED, THERE'S FINALLY SOME EXCITEMENT AROUND HERE.

SPEAKING OF YOUR COUSINS...
THEY'VE GOTTEN SO MOODY SINCE LAST YEAR!

I KNOW, RIGHT.

OH! DO YOU WANT ME TO SHOW YOU SOMETHING INTERESTING?

UHH...

ACTUALLY. I SHOULD GO BACK TO BED...
OF COURSE!

WOULDN'T WANT TO KEEP YOU UP.

GOOD NIGHT.

MAYBE I'LL SEE YOU TOMORROW?

...AND JUST SO YOU KNOW

WE GHOSTS, WE DON'T USUALLY HIDE IN THE BLIND SPOTS OF A ROOM...

I JUST WAIT FOR A GOOD TIME TO COME AND SAY "HELLO!"
AH. UM... OKAY...

LYDIA?

MMM...

WHAT NOW?!

ER...

NU – IT'S NOTHING...

URRR!
Huff!

BRRRR
BRRRRRR

WILL THAT DOG EVER SHUT UP?!

CAN YOU BE OUR LOOKOUT AND KEEP AN EYE OUT FOR GRANDMA?

UGH, BUT IT'S SO BORING!

DON'T YOU WANT ME TO FORGIVE YOU FOR RUINING OUR EVENING YESTERDAY?

AND THAT GUY WAS COOL, TOO.
YEAH, REALLY COOL.

WHAT'S GOING ON?
WHAT'S STOPPING YOU FROM
KEEPING WATCH?

HELLO!

YOU SEE, I APPEARED WHEN I WAS STILL FAR AWAY SO I DIDN'T SCARE YOU.
OH THAT WAS VERY... UH... THOUGHTFUL.

DO YOU WANT TO PLAY BADMINTON?

CAN YOU PASS THE JOINT?

COUGH COUGH!
YOU INHALED TOO MUCH...

YES, OKAY.

LOOK – YOU JUST PUFF ON IT.

OOPS, SORRY.

DON'T WORRY ABOUT FETCHING IT.

SWIF!

THAT'S SO COOL!

HAHA!

WHEW! I'VE GOT TO TAKE A BREAK!

SORRY. I FORGOT THAT YOU GET TIRED.

CAN I ASK YOU A QUESTION?

OF COURSE.

IF YOU'RE A GHOST...

THEN HOW COME YOU CAN TOUCH THINGS?

AH. WELL, THAT DEPENDS.
ON WHAT?

OKAY, SO...

SOMETIMES, I'M CORPOREAL, LIKE YOU.

AND SOMETIMES I'M NOT.

LOUISE?

WANNA COME TO THE BEACH?

UH... LIKE, RIGHT THIS SECOND?
YEAH, NOW!

OK!

THEN AGAIN...
YOU WERE A TERRIBLE LOOKOUT!

♫ LA LA LA ♪

MR JEKYLL...

IS EVERYTHING OKAY?
IT'S ABOUT YOUR DOG.
SOMETHING REALLY OUGHT TO BE DONE ABOUT HIM.

HE WOKE ME UP AGAIN LAST NIGHT.
I'M SORRY ABOUT THAT, BUT IT'S DIFFICULT TO STOP HIM BARKING.
THERE ARE SPECIAL COLLARS DESIGNED FOR THAT.
ABSOLUTELY OUT OF THE QUESTION! WE'VE DISCUSSED THIS BEFORE AND THERE'S NO WAY I'M MAKING HIM WEAR A COLLAR THAT GIVES HIM ELECTRIC SHOCKS!
HE WON'T HAVE TO WEAR IT FOR VERY LONG. DOGS ARE QUICK TO MAKE THE CONNECTION BETWEEN THEIR BARKING AND THE SHOCKS...
AND HOW ABOUT, INSTEAD, I GET YOU A NICE PAIR OF EARPLUGS?

LET'S GET YOU SOMETHING
TO EAT, LITTLE RASCAL.

woof woof!
ARGH! JUST WAIT ONE
MORE MINUTE!
WOOF WOOF!

SCREEEE

SCREEEEEEEEE

HMM. I'M GETTING DÉJA VU!

SO?

HOW WAS THE BEACH?

ERR... IT WAS OKAY, THANKS.

SORRY GIRLS, BUT WITH THAT GROUCH NEXT DOOR...

I'D FEEL MUCH BETTER IF YOU STAYED HERE TONIGHT.

SMACK!

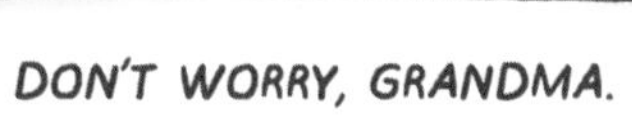
DON'T WORRY, GRANDMA.

squish!
WE UNDERSTAND.

WHO'S THE DOGGY THAT JUST CAN'T STOP BARKING?

I CAN SEE YOU, LOUISE! COME BACK AND HELP BRING IN THE DISHES.

SHE HAS IDENTIFIED
THE LEADERS OF
THE GANG...
TV
7 days

AND SHE'S FOLLOWING THEIR EVERY MOVE.

HOW DO YOU LIKE MY FEET IN YOUR FACE?

YEAHHHH! I LOOOVE IT...!

HERE'S WHAT WE'RE GOING TO DO TO STOP RODIN FROM BARKING THE HOUSE DOWN. WE'RE GOING TO LEAVE A SANDWICH IN THE KITCHEN AND THEN SNEAK OUT...

GOOD NIGHT!
CLICK!

NIGHT!

Z
Z

C'MON, BOY!
SANDWICH!
TIC! TIC! T

HAHAHA!

HAHAHA!

CRUNCH
CRUNCH!

CRUNCH!

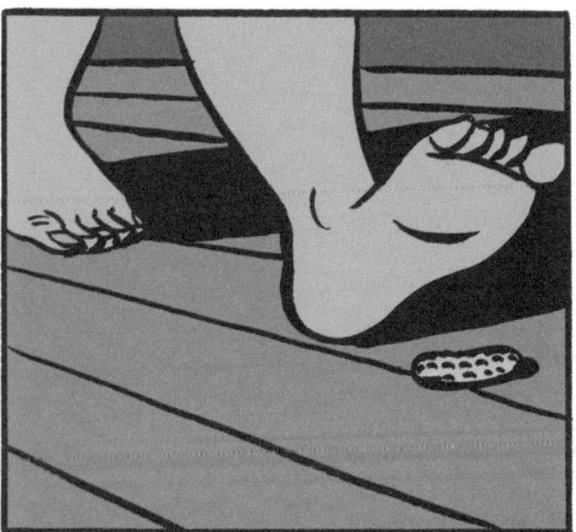
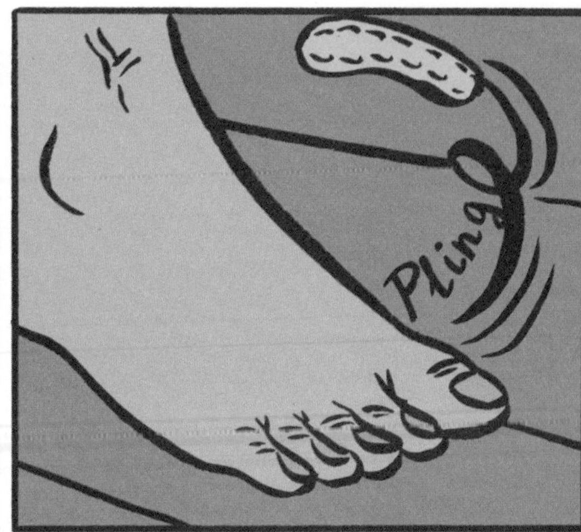
Pling

click!

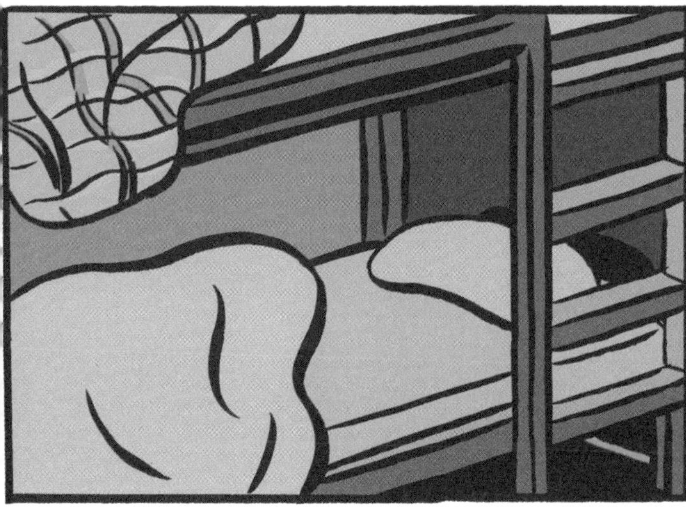

SO THE TEACHER WAS LIKE "OH REALLY, IS THAT WHY YOUR EYES ARE BLOODSHOT?"
HMM...

GIVE ME A MINUTE.
SO, NOUR...

CAN I SIT WITH YOU GUYS?
SURE!

AH SHIT!

GULP

HEY, GRANDMA! IT'S WAY PAST YOUR BEDTIME!

HAHAHA!

DO YOU NEED ANY HELP?

PISS OFF, LOUISE!

WHY DO YOU TALK TO HER LIKE THAT?

WHY DO YOU THINK?

DO YOU REALLY THINK GRANDMA WOKE UP LAST NIGHT OF HER OWN ACCORD?

THAT'S TRUE. SHE USUALLY SLEEPS LIKE A LOG...

AH-HA! I JUST FOUND SOME MARMALADE THAT EXPIRED SIX YEARS AGO!
HAHAHA!

TIC!

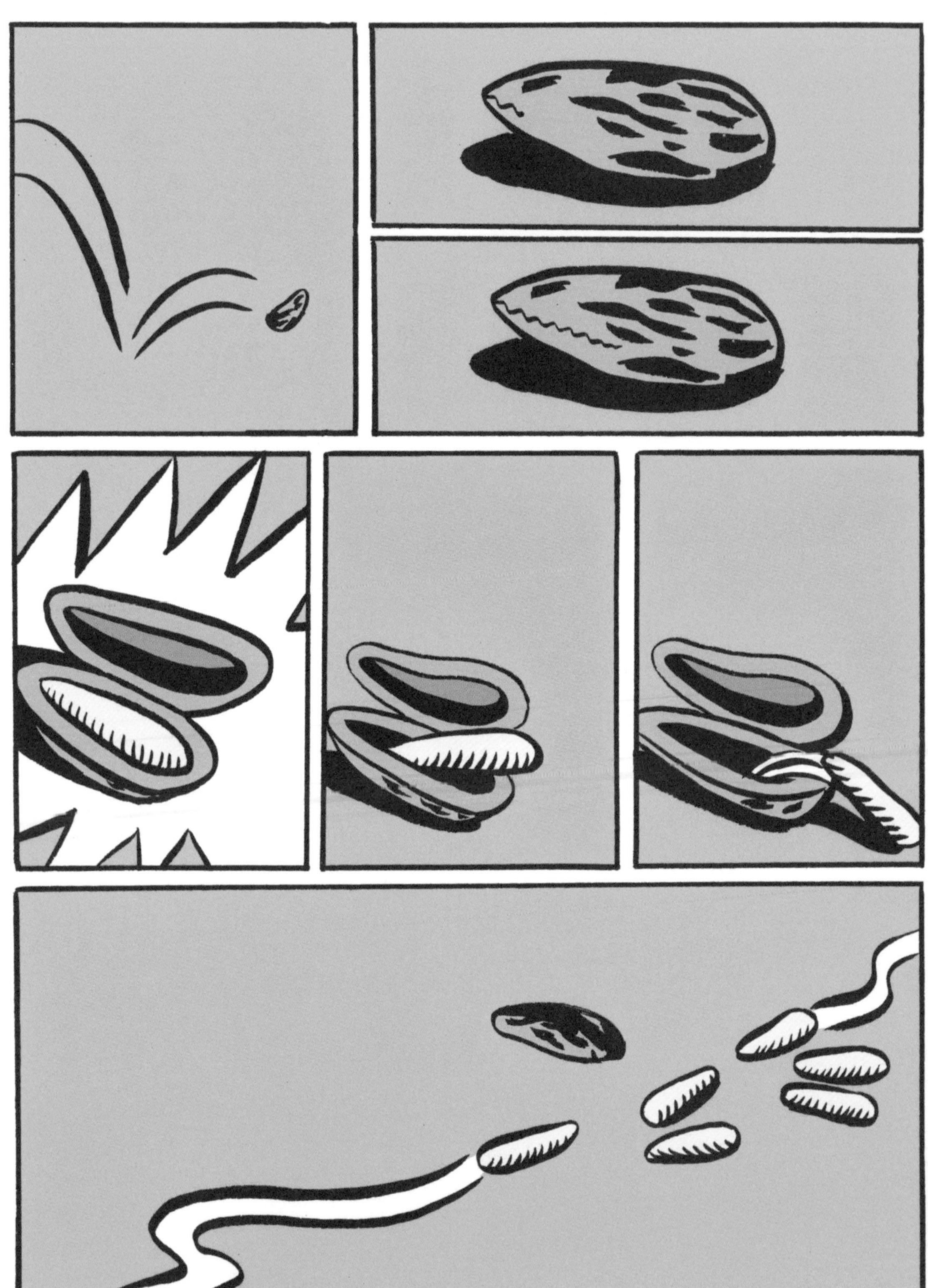

OH, HI LISA. IT'S WEIRDLY SATISFYING BASHING UP THESE PINE CONES.

WHAT HAPPENED?
ARE YOU UPSET?
SORRY, IT'S NOTHING
TO DO WITH YOU.

IT'S A LOVELY DAY. ARE YOU SURE YOU WANT TO SPEND IT SULKING?

OR DO YOU WANT ME TO SHOW YOU SOMETHING?

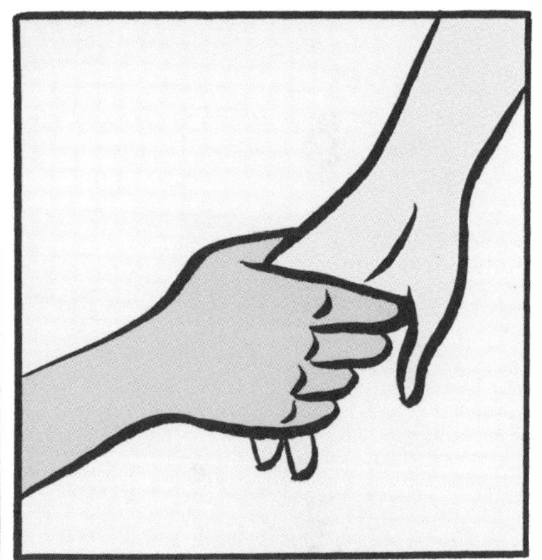

YOUR HAND FEELS SO WARM...

HAHA!
WHAT DID YOU THINK GHOSTS ARE SUPPOSED TO FEEL LIKE?

FOLLOW ME, THIS WAY!

THAT'S WEIRD, I DON'T REMEMBER COMING TO THIS PART OF THE GARDEN BEFORE.

ARE YOU COMING?

The other side of the mirror
FRIDAY

SCROOGE MCDUCK

GUESS WHO?

OH!

IT WAS YOU THAT PINCHED THIS FROM ME ON MY FIRST NIGHT, WASN'T IT?

SORRY!

IT'S JUST SO FASCINATING TO ME!

ALL THAT DETAIL AND THE STRANGE MATERIAL...
PLASTIC.

YOU'RE SO LUCKY. WHEN I WAS ALIVE, WE DIDN'T HAVE TOYS LIKE THIS.

THAT'S FUNNY, GRANDMA ALWAYS SAYS YOU DIDN'T HAVE ANY TOYS AT ALL.

"YOU GIRLS ARE SO SPOILED! BACK IN MY DAY, WE HAD ONE PINE CONE TO PLAY WITH...
...AND WE WERE LUCKY TO EVEN GET THAT!"

SHE WAS LYING!

IT'S BECAUSE SHE WOULD HAVE LOVED TO HAVE HAD TOYS LIKE YOURS.
HAHA!

GUESS WHO?
DO YOU WANT TO PLAY GUESS WHO?

OH... WHAT HAPPENED TO THE CHARACTERS?
OH YES! SO IN THE ORIGINAL GAME...

I DIDN'T LIKE THAT THERE WERE SO FEW GIRLS, OR THE WAY THAT NONE OF THEM HAD MOUSTACHES.
FRANK
SOPHIE
DANIEL

SO I DECIDED TO MAKE NEW ONES FOR MYSELF...
AND INVENT NEW SPECIES: ALIENS, HALF-ANIMAL AND HALF-HUMANS...

DO YOU WANT TO MAKE SOME, TOO?

LOUUISEEEE!!!!!

DINNER
TiiiME!!!!!

HEY!
HOW WOULD YOU LIKE TO COME TO THE BEACH WITH ME TOMORROW?

UM... I CAN'T. BUT THANKS FOR ASKING!

LOUIIISE!

WHERE HAVE YOU BEEN HIDING?
JUST THE GARDEN!

?

THANK YOU, LYDIA!

IT'S NICE TO BE WAITED ON.

AND SOPHIE, THE SALAD YOU MADE IS SO GOOD!

DOES THIS MEAN YOU'RE NOT UPSET WITH US AFTER LAST NIGHT?

WHY WOULD I BE?

...

...

NO REASON, GRANDMA...

NO REASON AT ALL.

RONCH
RONC
NC

ARGH!
NOUR!

HAHAHA!

...YOU WILL FIND OUT IN
KOH LANTA!

OH GOSH!

THE MOSQUITOES
MUST LOVE YOU!

WILL YOU COME WITH ME TO THE BEACH TOMORROW AFTERNOON?

OH LOOK!
HOW CUTE IS THAT SQUIRREL!

HEY!
Splush!

PRI

WOULD YOU LIKE ANY OLIVES?

shpout

shpout

YOU HAVEN'T TORN OFF THE DATES FROM YOUR CALENDAR FOR TEN DAYS!
16th AUGUST
REALLY?

CAN I ASK YOU A QUESTION?

WHY DON'T YOU EVER COME TO THE BEACH?
get ready for next week's issue !

IF YOU TELL ME...

I'LL LET YOU BORROW MY TROLL FOR THE WHOLE DAY!

I DON'T NEED YOUR PERMISSION TO TAKE IT.

THERE'S NO REASON TO GET CRABBY!
SORRY.

OKAY, FINE. I'LL TRY TO EXPLAIN...

IF I GO BEYOND THE BOUNDARIES OF THE HOUSE...

I CEASE TO EXIST.

BUT... AREN'T YOU ALREADY A SPIRIT?
YES. BUT WHAT I MEAN IS...

MY CONSCIOUSNESS, MY THOUGHTS...

COMPLETELY DISAPPEAR.

SO YOU'D PREFER TO BE
BORED STIFF — HERE? FOREVER?

SURE, IT'S NOT QUITE THE SAME AS BEING ALIVE...

...BUT I'D TAKE THAT OVER OBLIVION ANY DAY.

ANYWAY THERE ARE LOADS OF AMAZING THINGS I CAN DO THAT I HAVEN'T SHOWN YOU YET.

FOR EXAMPLE, YOU SEE THAT SQUIRREL?

YES.

IF I WANT, I CAN ENTER HIS MIND...

HUH?
HOW'D YOU DO THAT?

LISA?

IS THAT REALLY YOU?

AMAZING...

HI THERE!

ARGH! OW!
STOP IT! YOU'RE SCRATCHING ME!

I SAID GET OFF!

GET OFF ME!

LET GO!

CLICK

Splash!

HI!

SUP, I GOT THE BOARD
I WAS TELLING YOU ABOUT...

YOU WANNA
SEE IT?

RIGHT ON!

IT'S THE NEXT ONE ALONG.

I HAVE TO ADMIT, WITH MY SUNGLASSES IT DIDN'T LOOK LIKE MUCH...

BUT SHE'S AWESOME...

ARE YOU SPYING?

COME ON YOU, ICE CREAM'S ON ME.

YOU KNOW, I'M TIRED OF ALL THIS DRAMA...

I DON'T WANT TO SEE OUR COUSINS' RELATIONSHIP RUINED OVER SOME GUY.

BUT HEY, WHAT ELSE CAN YOU DO WITH ALL THOSE RAGING HORMONES?

FUUUUUCK...
I'M GOING TO SHUT UP...

SO I CAN EAT THIS ICE CREAM BEFORE IT MELTS!

WAIT! LET ME EXPLAIN!

EXPLAIN WHAT?

"DEAR VIEWERS,
OUR SUMMER SPECIAL WILL BEGIN SOON!"

"HOW WILL LYDIA REACT WHEN SHE DISCOVERS THE BUDDING ROMANCE BETWEEN THE HOT GUY AT THE BEACH AND HER OWN COUSIN?"

YOU STOLE THE ONLY GUY I HAVE EVER BEEN IN LOVE WITH!

I HAVE **NOTHING** ELSE TO SAY TO YOU!

IN LOVE?

DON'T YOU THINK YOU'RE EXAGGERATING JUST A BIT?

YOU CAN'T LOVE SOMEONE ONLY FOR THEIR LOOKS, YOU KNOW!
THAT'S LUCKY FOR YOU!

GASP

THAT WAS A REALLY NASTY THING TO SAY!

THAT'S RIGHT! WALK AWAY! YOU COWARD!

"WHY DID YOU KISS ME?"
"BECAUSE I LIKED YOU FROM THE FIRST TIME I SAW YOU."

Zzzzlip!

RELAX, LYDIA.
YOU WERE SMOKING.

IT CAN DEFINITELY
MAKE YOU SEE THINGS...

SCROOGE
MCDUCK

Dr SLUMP

DID YOU HAVE FUN
SCARING MY SISTER?

OVER THE YEARS, I'VE SEEN LOTS OF PRETTY GIRLS COME TO THE HOUSE...

AND ALMOST WITHOUT EXCEPTION, IT'S THE SAME OLD STORY...

BECAUSE OF THEIR BEAUTY...

THE WORLD BELONGS TO THEM...

...FOR A WHILE.

THEN ONE DAY, THEY REALISE THAT THEY'VE BASED THEIR ENTIRE LIVES ON ONE THING.

FANEL
GETTING BY ON THEIR MOST SUPERFICIAL QUALITY — THEIR PHYSICAL APPEARANCE.

WHILE THEY COULD HAVE BEEN IMPROVING AND ENHANCING SO MANY OTHER ASPECTS OF THEIR LIVES.

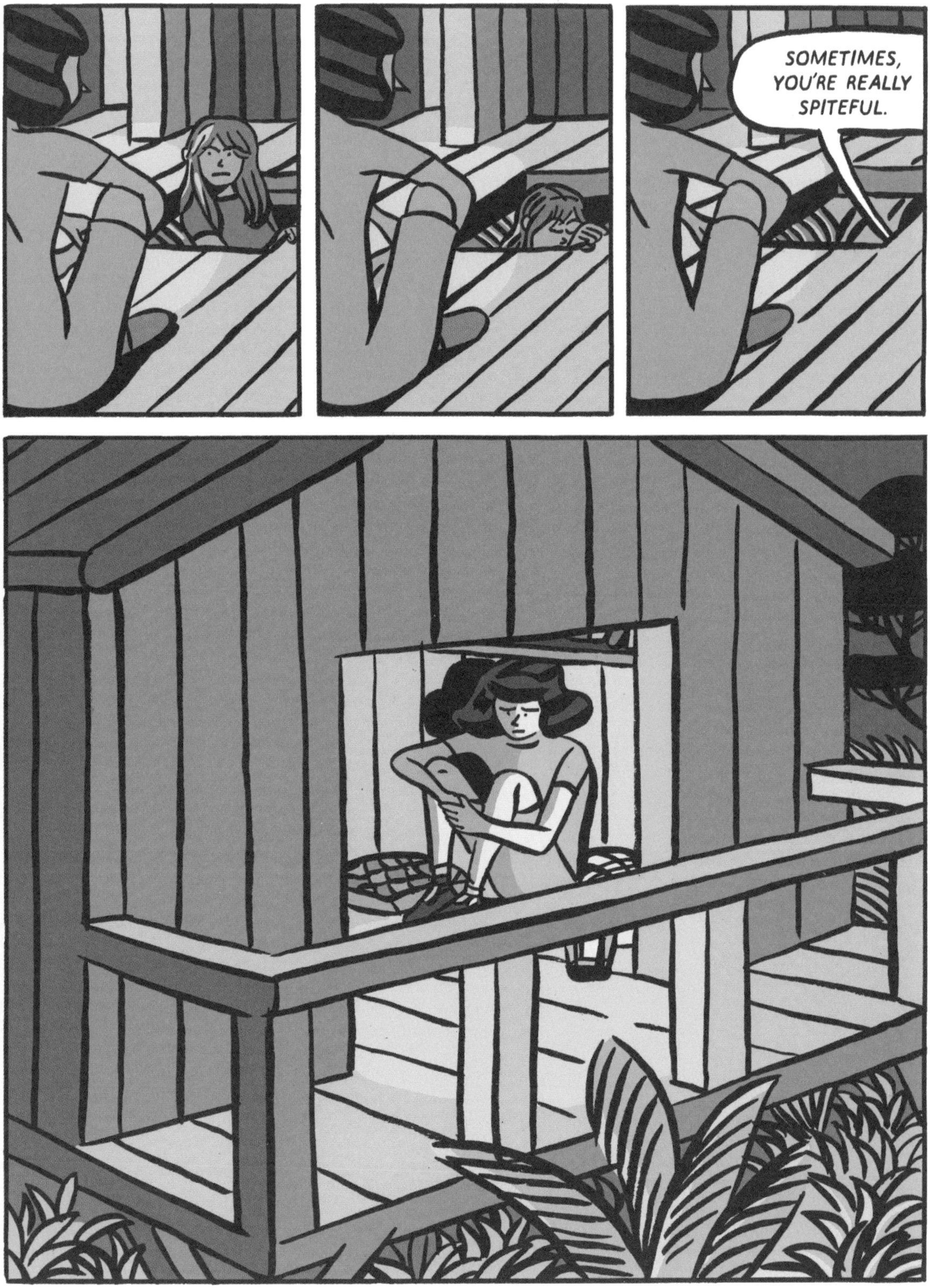

SOMETIMES, YOU'RE REALLY SPITEFUL.

Flip
Flop!

ARE WE GOING TO THE BEACH LATER?

POC
POC

AHA!
RUMMY!

WOW! THE TENSION AT THIS TABLE...

HOW MUCH LONGER ARE YOU GOING TO SULK FOR?

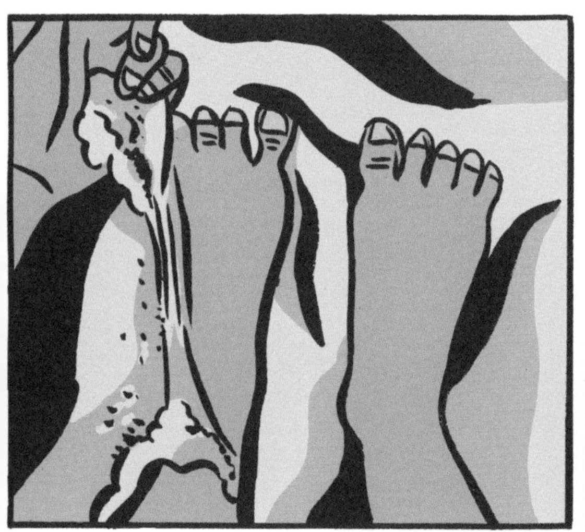

AREN'T YOU COMING
UP WITH US?
NO, I'M GOING TO
HANG UP MY TOWEL.

LISA?

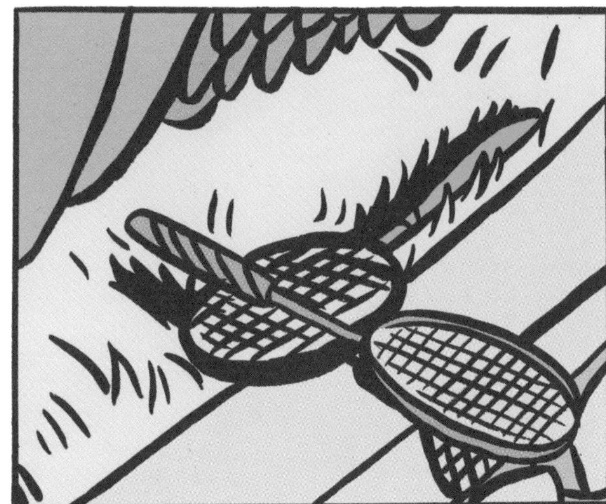

CAWWW

CAWWW
CAWWWW

HAHAHA!

GREAT DISGUISE!

BUT I KNOW IT'S YOU!

HUFF PUFF

HELLO!

WHERE HAVE YOU BEEN?

SORRY...

I'VE BEEN BUSY TURNING MYSELF INTO...

A TEENAGER.

SMOOCH!

HAHA! GROSS!

SERIOUSLY, THOUGH...

NEXT TIME, LET ME KNOW WHEN YOU'RE PLANNING TO DISAPPEAR.

BECAUSE I'M LEAVING IN A WEEK...

IS IT POSSIBLE FOR YOU TO LEAVE THE BOUNDARIES OF THE HOUSE THROUGH THE SKY?

SADLY NOT...

"I CAN ONLY FLY AROUND
INSIDE THE BOUNDARIES."

HOO
HOO...

flap!

SCRONTCH
SCRONTCH

I WONDER WHAT THAT FEELS LIKE...
WHAT? EATING A MOUSE?

EW, NO. TO FLY...

AH, YOU FEEL ALL YOUR FEATHERS VIBRATE: BRRRRR!

HAHAHA! NO, I'M JUST KIDDING.

WANT TO GIVE IT A TRY?

DON'T BE SCARED...

JUST RELAX!

EASY FOR YOU TO SAY!

TRY TO REALLY
LOOSEN UP.

PFF!
PFF!
PFF!

THERE YOU GO, JUST LIKE THAT.

WOOHOO!

RODIN!

WOOF WOOF!

MWAH ♡

PSST!

slurp!

ARGH!
GROSS!

WHAT IS SHE DOING IN THERE?

BANG BANG BANG
LOUIIISE!
DO YOU HAVE YOUR SWIMSUIT ON OR NOT?

OKAY, OKAY! I'M READY!

clack!

THE WAY THEY WALK IS SO WEIRD!

NO WEIRDER THAN US...
?

SO, LOUISE?

LOOKS LIKE YOU AND THAT CRAB WERE FINALLY HITTING IT OFF.
VERY FUNNY!

le club
TROPIC
COKTAIL
7€ !

HEY, NOUR! LISTEN TO THIS BIT...

"WHILE ON A BOARD, ONE IS TRULY FREE FROM LAND-BOUND RESTRICTIONS."
"FOR THAT HOUR HE IS THE CAPTAIN OF HIS FATE, OF HIS MINIATURE SHIP..."

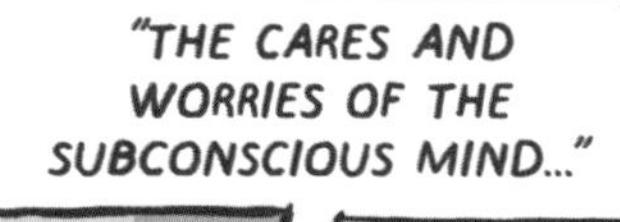
"THE CARES AND WORRIES OF THE SUBCONSCIOUS MIND..."

"ARE ERASED AND FORGOTTEN..."

"UNTIL THE TENSIONS OF THE LIVING AGAIN BUILD UP."

COOL...

WANT TO GO FOR A SWIM?

LAST ONE TO THE BUOY IS A LOSER!

HAHA! I BEAT YOU!

smack!

ER... WHAT DID YOU JUST DO?

WELL, I'M LEAVING.

OH, AREN'T YOU HUNGRY?

OR DID I ALREADY GIVE YOU YOUR FOOD TONIGHT?

BLOODY HELL!
I CAN'T BELIEVE THAT I DIDN'T REMEMBER!

"...ANOTHER LARGE-SCALE SHIPWRECK OFF THE COAST OF SICILY..."

OW!
EXCUSE ME...
"INITIAL FIGURES ARE 26 DEATHS, 53 INJURED AND AT LEAST 60 MISSING."

"DESPITE CONTINGENCY PLANS BEING LAUNCHED ACROSS EUROPE, THE MEDITERRANEAN HAS BECOME A CEMETERY FOR HUNDREDS OF MIGRANTS EVERY YEAR."

YOU SEE!
THERE ARE MORE IMPORTANT THINGS THAN YOUR SCHOOLGIRL DRAMAS!

DO THEY HAVE A PONYTAIL?
YES.

IT'S TERRY!
YOU WIN!

IT'S ANNOYING...
WHAT IS?

IT'S WHEN YOU'RE HAVING THE MOST FUN...

...THAT YOU KNOW THE VACATION IS COMING TO AN END.

...

YOU KNOW ...

YOU COULD STAY...

OH REALLY?
HOW'S THAT?

NO, NOTHING.

FORGET I SAID ANYTHING...

NO WAY!
TELL ME WHAT YOU MEAN.

WELL... IT SEEMS TO ME THAT YOU'RE NOT LOOKING FORWARD TO BEING A TEENAGER.

BUT YOU COULD MAKE IT SO YOU NEVER HAVE TO GROW UP.

AND NEVER HAVE TO DO ANYTHING EXCEPT PLAY AND FLY.

BUT TO DO THAT...

I'D HAVE TO DIE FIRST, RIGHT?

SO?

WOULD THAT BE SO BAD?

WE ARE NEVER ANYTHING MORE THAN DUST.

ARGH!

ALL THE TIME WE'VE SPENT TOGETHER HASN'T BEEN ENOUGH FOR YOU?

YOU HAD TO SPY ON ME, TOO?

EXCUSE ME?

"I NEVER SAID I DIDN'T WANT TO GROW UP."

ARGH!
GROSS!

WHAT IS SHE DOING
IN THERE?

LOUiiiSE!

OKAY, OKAY!
I'M READY!

OH, YOU HAVEN'T ASKED FOR YOUR BREAKFAST YET!
DAILY TIMES
Deadly forest fires

THAT'S NOT LIKE YOU! YOU'RE NOT LOOKING TOO GOOD, MY BOY...

IF YOU'RE NOT FEELING BETTER SOON, I'M CALLING THE VET.

ARGH!

YOU SCARED ME, LOUISE!
SORRY...
COULD I COME WITH YOU TO THE MARKET TODAY?
OF COURSE.

DO YOU WANT SOME OLIVES?

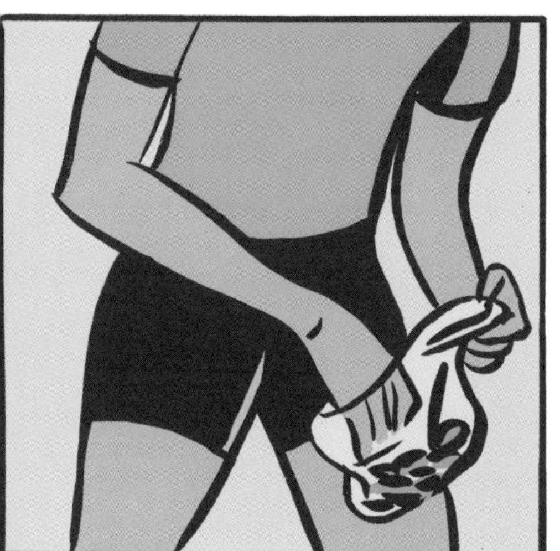

MMMM

LET'S GO AND
GET SOME FISH.

FISHMONGER

WOULD YOU LIKE SOME OLIVES, LOUISE?

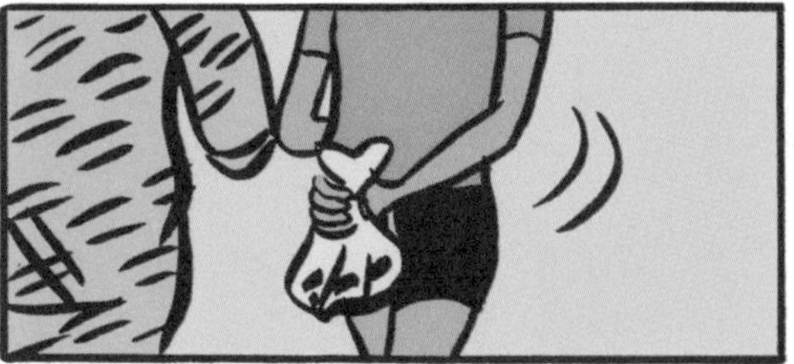

NO, THANKS!

I'VE ALWAYS LIVED IN THIS HOUSE, YOU SEE.

ALL MY MEMORIES ARE IN THESE WALLS.

I WATCHED MY SISTER AND MY PARENTS DIE IN THIS HOUSE. BUT I ALSO GAVE BIRTH TO ALL OF MY CHILDREN HERE.

YOUR SISTER LISA?
YES.

HOW DID SHE DIE?

WELL...

OF COURSE IT'S HARD FOR ME TO MAINTAIN A HOUSE LIKE THIS BY MYSELF...

BUT I LOVE IT.

HMM... HAVE YOU NOTICED?

RODIN'S NOT BARKING.

SOMETHING'S NOT RIGHT.

WHEW! AHH! PFF! THESE DAMN STAIRS!

I'M TAKING YOU STRAIGHT TO THE VET.

LOUISE —

INSTEAD OF COMING IN THE CAR...
CLICK!

GO AND OPEN THE GATE FOR ME.

WAIT, GRANDMA!
I'M COMING WITH YOU.

THE BEST THING WE CAN DO IS KEEP RODIN IN FOR THE DAY...

...SO WE CAN RUN SOME TESTS.

MIND HOW YOU GO! I'LL CALL YOU THIS EVENING.
DÉTART

ARE YOU OKAY, GRANDMA?

WELL?
THE VET DOESN'T KNOW WHAT'S WRONG WITH HIM. SHE'S GOING TO CALL ME LATER ON.

WOULD YOU LIKE US TO STAY WITH YOU TODAY?

NO, NO! IT'S YOUR LAST DAY – GO TO THE BEACH!

THEN AFTER ALL THIS DRAMA IS OVER, I'LL GO AND GET ANOTHER LITTLE DOG...

ISN'T THAT RIGHT, LOUISE?
HAHA! VERY FUNNY!

LOUISE, WE HAVE TO GO NOW.

I JUST WANT TO FINISH SOMETHING...

HEY! GIRLS!

RIIIIINNNG!
AH, DARN!
THE VET!

TAKE THE LAUNDRY
FOR ME, LOUISE!

RIIIIIING

RODIN DIED.

WHAT HAPPENED?
HE ATE A PIECE OF GLASS ONE OR TWO DAYS AGO.

AND IT PERFORATED HIS STOMACH.

HI!
ARE YOU AVOIDING ME?

NOT AT ALL!
THEN HOW COME YOU HAVEN'T BEEN AT THE HOUSE ALL DAY?

I JUST WANTED TO ENJOY MY LAST DAY HERE AT THE BEACH.

YOU KNOW...

YOU DON'T HAVE TO GO ALL THE WAY TO THE BEACH TO SWIM.

SEE?

I SEE.

CAN'T TELL IF IT'S REAL...

Squelch
Squelch

LYDIA! LOUISE!!!

YOUR MOTHER IS HERE!!!!!!!

ARE YOU OKAY, MUM?

WELL, YES. HE WAS JUST A DOG...

ROBIN

HELLO.

I HAVE SOMETHING FOR YOU...

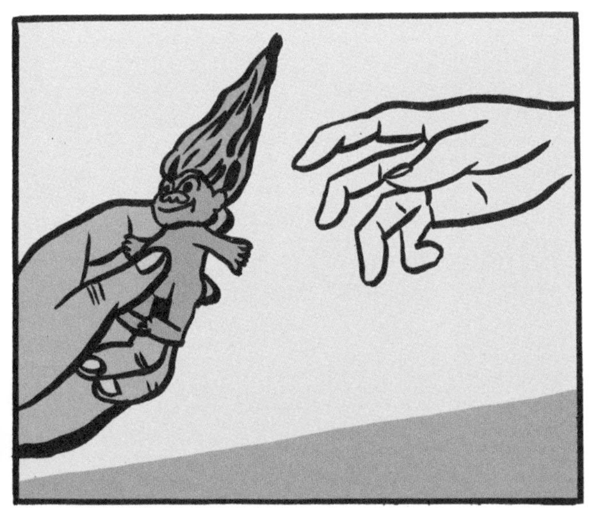

ARE YOU SURE?

OF COURSE! I HAVE ANOTHER ONE AT MY PARENTS' HOUSE.

THIS WAY, WE BOTH HAVE SOMETHING TO REMIND EACH OTHER OF THIS SUMMER.

GOODBYE, LISA.

HUH? THIS LADDER IS GOING ON FOREVER!

ARGH!

PLEASE, LISA...

STOP IT!

UGH,
NEVER MIND.

I'VE GOT PLENTY
OF TIME!

zzzlip!

BOF!

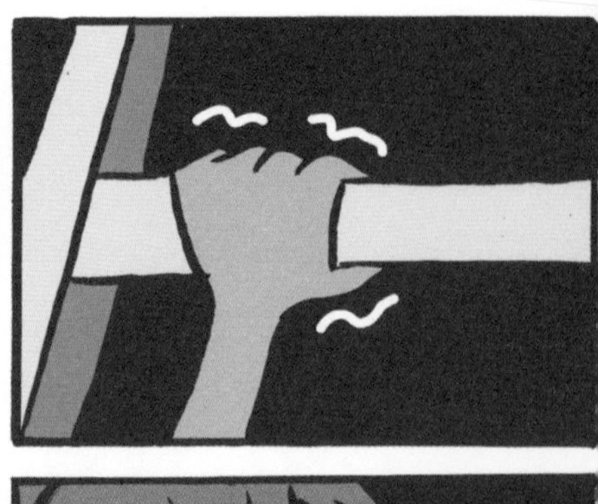

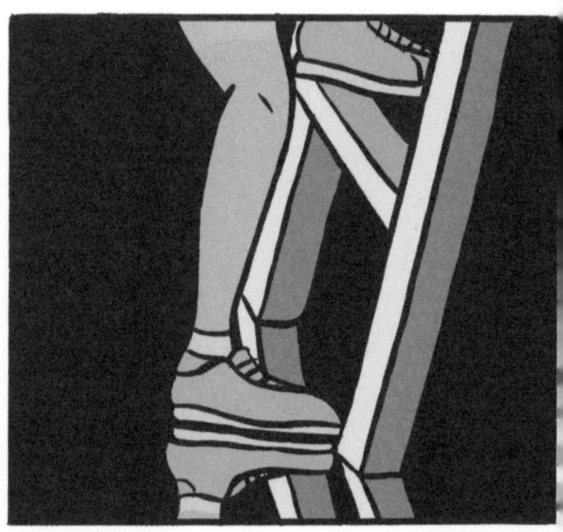

TELL HER TO BRING DOWN HER SUITCASE!
OKAY!

OH! LOUISE...
YOU'RE HERE!

OH, SWEETIE... YOU'RE UPSET ABOUT RODIN.

COME ON, YOU. LET'S GET YOUR THINGS TOGETHER AND GO HOME.

CLICK!

BYE.
BYE.

LOUISE, WHEN WE GET HOME
I'M TAKING YOU FOR A HAIRCUT!

MUM?

YES,
KITTEN?

IN THE GARDEN
AT GRANDMA'S...
WAS THERE EVER
A TREE HOUSE?

WHY DO YOU ASK?

SIGH

OKAY.

YOU'RE NOT A LITTLE GIRL ANYMORE...

I'LL TELL YOU.

THERE WAS A TREE HOUSE IN THE GARDEN...
BUT IT WAS A LONG TIME AGO.

HAHA!
WHEN YOUR GRANDMA WAS LITTLE.

LISA!
Juliet!
BACK THEN, SHE AND HER SISTER DROVE MY GRANDMA MAD!

GET ONE FOR ME!

WHAT ON EARTH HAVE THEY BEEN DOING?

YOUR BRAND NEW DRESSES!!

WHACK

BUT IT TOOK MORE THAN A TELLING-OFF OR A SMACK TO DISHEARTEN THE LITTLE GIRLS.

THE DRESS IS ITCHING ME!
Pff pff!
IT'S REMINDING YOU WHAT A MESS YOU MADE OF IT YESTERDAY!

READY... NOW DON'T MOVE!

click!

FIRST ONE TO THE TREE HOUSE WINS!

zzzip!

KRRR

HUFF
HUFF

KRAAK!

Thwack!
THE TREE HOUSE...

THE OLD TREE...

MY GRANDPA CUT IT ALL DOWN.

SOME YEARS LATER, THAT PART OF THE GARDEN WAS SOLD OFF AND A WALL WAS PUT UP.

...AND IT BECAME THE GARDEN YOU KNOW TODAY.

Click!

RODIN

ROBIN

ROBIN

woof
woof!